Goldilocks and the Three Bears

ILLUSTRATED BY RICHARD DEVERELL

Story adapted by
Christine Deverell

There were once upon a time three bears who lived very happily together in a charming little house in the middle of the woods. There was a Little Baby Bear, a Mother Bear and a Big Father Bear.

Each had a bowl for its porridge – a tiny bowl for the Little Baby Bear, a medium sized bowl for Mother Bear, and a great big bowl for the Big Father Bear.

Each had a chair to sit on – a tiny chair for the Little Baby Bear, a medium sized chair for Mother Bear and a great big chair for the Big Father Bear.

Each had a bed to sleep in – a tiny bed for the Little Baby Bear, a medium sized bed for Mother Bear and a great big bed for the Big Father Bear.

One day, after they had made the porridge for their breakfast, they decided to go for a walk to give the porridge time to cool down. While they were out, a little girl named Goldilocks passed the house.

She peered through the windows and peeped through the keyhole. Seeing that no one was home, she lifted the latch and went inside.

She saw the bowls of
porridge on the breakfast table and
not having eaten yet, decided to help
herself. She tried Big Father Bear's
porridge, but that was too salty for
her. Then she tried
some of Mother Bear's
porridge, but that was
too sweet. Next she
tried Little Baby Bear's

porridge, and that was just right; neither too salty, nor too

sweet, and she ate it all up.

Then Goldilocks sat down in Big Father Bear's

chair. It was much too hard, so she

tried Mother

Bear's chair.

That was

much too

soft. So next she tried Little Baby

Bear's chair, and it felt perfect.

But Goldilocks was just a little too big

for Little Baby Bear's chair, and after she

had sat in it

for a few

seconds,

the leg broke, and Goldilocks

crashed to the floor!

After all this, Goldilocks

felt rather tired so she went upstairs, hoping to find a

comfortable bed to have a little rest on. First of all she lay

down on Big Father Bear's bed.

However, that was

much too hard

for her liking,

so next she

tried Mother

Bear's bed,

but that was

much too soft.

So she tried Little Baby Bear's bed, and it felt just perfect.

She got right under the covers and fell fast asleep.

While she slept, the three bears came home for their breakfast. Goldilocks had made quite a mess on the table.

"Who's been eating my porridge?" boomed Big Father Bear in his great, gruff voice.

"Who's been eating my porridge?" said Mother Bear in her cross voice. "And who's been eating my porridge?" cried

Little Baby Bear in his squeaky little voice, "And they've eaten it all up!"

They looked around the room and saw that the furniture had been moved. They went over to their chairs. "Who's been sitting on my chair?" boomed Big Father Bear in his great, gruff voice, for Goldilocks had used the hard cushion to wipe the porridge off her fingers. "Who's been sitting on my chair?" said Mother Bear in her cross voice, for Goldilocks had left a big dent in the soft cushion. "And who's been sitting on my chair?" cried Little Baby Bear in his

squeaky little voice. "And they've broken it!" By now poor
Little Baby Bear was in tears.

Together the three bears went upstairs to the bedroom.
First, they came to Big Father Bear's bed. "Who's been lying
on my bed?" boomed Big Father Bear in his great, gruff voice,
for Goldilocks had crumpled the sheets. "Who's been lying
on my bed?" said Mother Bear in her cross voice, for
Goldilocks had thrown the soft pillows onto the floor, and
left a dirty mark on the fine quilt.

"And who is that sleeping in my bed?" cried Little

19

Baby Bear in his squeaky little voice through his tears. "Look! She ate my porridge! She broke my chair! She made a mess in our house! And now, there she is! She's sleeping in my bed!"

Suddenly, Goldilocks woke up and saw the three bears staring down at her crossly. She sprung out of the bed and sped down the stairs, out of the front door and into the woods. The three bears heard Goldilocks crying out: "There are bears in the woods! Help! Help! There are bears in the woods!" Her voice faded into silence, and the three bears were never bothered by her again.

20